why we wrote this book

Leadership can be learned at any age and children begin to pick up leadership skills early in life. We are leadership consultants and have four children and six grandchildren between us. As we raised and advised our own children, we heard so many stories that we decided to put them in a book for parents to read to their children. Together, you can discuss and learn essential lessons about how to act like a leader. The stories cover different topics, but the message is that a child can be a leader *anytime* and *anywhere*. We hope you enjoy this book as much as we enjoyed writing it and that your children can use the stories to shape their own leadership as they grow and develop.

Molly and Peter

meet our Little Leaders

Miranda is athletic and outgoing and loves her cat Ginger. She enjoys being with her friends and she loves banana pancakes.

Lily is new at their school this year and would like to make more friends. She plays the flute and likes to bake cookies with her mom.

Marco is small and shy. He likes to sing and his favorite song is the Beatles' "All You Need is Love." He always wears his blue backpack.

Carter is the tallest boy in his class and wishes more of his friends had freckles like he does. He loves to talk and tell stories to his friends.

TJ's favorite sport is soccer, and he likes history a lot. His favorite ice cream is red, white and blueberry. He loves to wear his red baseball cap.

Marco is the smallest in his first grade class and is very shy – especially when the teacher calls on him. Even when he knows the answer, he can't seem to find the right words.

One day he was asked to read a short poem in class. He took a deep breath and said to himself, "I can do this." He stood up and did a great job reading the poem.

Little Leaders find the courage to do their best even when they are afraid.

TJ saw Miranda sitting alone on a bench in the playground looking sad.
He went over and asked her what was wrong.

She told him her brother was sick and she began to cry. He sat down and listened quietly until she felt better, and he and his dog Puck helped to cheer her up.

Little Leaders show empathy and compassion to those around them.

Carter was walking down the hall when he saw William, a classmate, opening Miranda's locker. William was looking inside and pulling things out.

Carter walked up to him and asked what he was doing. William's face turned red and he had no answer. Carter told him to stop and leave Miranda's things alone.

Little Leaders respect other people's stuff and don't touch things without permission.

Carter and Lily ran to the playground where they saw Marco being bullied by some older kids. It didn't look good. They came closer and saw someone push Marco and call him a name. Lily said to Carter,

"We have to help."

Both Carter and Lily went over and asked the older kids to leave Marco alone.

Lily told them "You are bigger than he is and that's not right."

Carter and Lily led Marco to safety.

Being a Little Leader means standing up when you see someone being bullied.

Marco was singing a song one day when he thought no one was listening. He liked to sing and had a great voice, and Carter heard him as he came up from behind.

Carter asked Marco to stand with him in the front row at their sing-a-long for grandparents. Marco was scared at first but agreed. Everyone complimented Marco on his voice, and his confidence grew.

Little Leaders help build the confidence of their friends by encouraging them and helping them overcome their fears.

Miranda never sat with Lily at lunch because she liked to sit with her other friends. One day she saw Lily sitting alone and felt badly.

Miranda went over and asked Lily to join her lunch group. The other girls were already at the table and they all ate and talked together.

Little Leaders are kind and thoughtful and try to include others.

Carter talked a lot outside of class. He interrupted his friends with his stories and they were getting tired of it and began to avoid him.

TJ took Carter aside one day and told him he needed to listen more and talk less, or he would lose friends. Carter thought about it and started listening more.

Little Leaders listen to others and don't interrupt when they are talking.

Lily and Miranda lived next door to each other and often played together after school. Miranda loved to ride her bike in their neighborhood, but Lily was scared. Miranda offered to help Lily learn to ride and she agreed.

Lily was still afraid and fell off a lot. Each time she fell, Miranda encouraged her to try again. Soon Lily was riding as well as Miranda.

Little Leaders are patient with friends who may not be able to do everything they can do.

TJ's father and grandfather were great soccer players and loved the game. TJ wanted to be as good as they were, so he practiced his foot skills and kicks every day – sometimes for hours.

When he finally was good enough to play his first game, he scored and his team won. He felt good and his family was there to cheer for him.

Little Leaders keep on trying and don't give up when they really want something.

Lily invited Miranda to a sleepover at her house and they were both excited about it. Then, another classmate invited Miranda to her birthday party, which was the same day and time. It sounded liked fun and she wanted to go.

Miranda thought about telling Lily she couldn't come to her house, but she realized how sad that would make Lily, who was not invited to the birthday party. It was hard but she turned down the birthday party invitation and went to Lily's house as they had planned.

Little Leaders keep their promises to their friends.

Carter was always polite to his teachers.
But, when he was at home he was often rude
and disrespectful, refusing to do his chores
and not listening to his mom.

TJ came over to his house and was surprised by his friend's behavior. He said something to Carter, who thought about it, and realized his parents were the most special people in his life.

Little Leaders treat their families with kindness and respect.

Miranda was a really good basketball player and loved shooting the ball and making baskets. She grabbed the ball whenever she could and almost never passed it to her teammates. They began to wish they had more turns at getting the ball.

One day, Miranda overheard her friends talking and realized that they didn't think she was a team player. Miranda recognized that she should help her teammates get better at the game and that she didn't always have to be the star.

Little leaders like to compete, but they include their friends, because teamwork is what wins the game.

Thank you for reading our stories!

To order additional copies of this book, contact:
Xlibris
844-714-8691
www.Xlibris.com
Orders@Xlibris.com

ISBN: Softcover   978-1-5434-9989-6
         Hardcover   978-1-5434-9990-2
         EBook   978-1-5434-9988-9

Library of Congress Control Number: 2021919770

Print information available on the last page

Rev. date: 09/30/2021

Printed in the United States
by Baker & Taylor Publisher Services